CW00858139

About the Authors

Brendan Tannam and Kate Tannam are husband and wife, originally from Dublin, Ireland. They now live in beautiful York, North England, with their football-mad son, Tadhg and baby daughter Alannah.

Brendan Tannam & Kate Tannam

Littlesville Tigers: Let the Games Begin

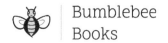

Bumblebee
Books

BUMBLEBEE PAPERBACK EDITION

Copyright © Brendan Tannam & Kate Tannam 2023

The right of Brendan Tannam & Kate Tannam to be identified as author of
this work has been asserted in accordance with sections 77 and 78 of the Copyright, Designs and
Patents Act 1988.

All Rights Reserved

No reproduction, copy or transmission of this publication
may be made without written permission.
No paragraph of this publication may be reproduced,
copied or transmitted save with the written permission of the publisher, or in accordance with the
provisions
of the Copyright Act 1956 (as amended).

Any person who commits any unauthorised act in relation to
this publication may be liable to criminal
prosecution and civil claims for damage.

A CIP catalogue record for this title is
available from the British Library.

ISBN: 978-1-83934-625-5

Bumblebee Books is an imprint of
Olympia Publishers.

First Published in 2023

Olympia Publishers
Tallis House
2 Tallis Street
London
EC4Y 0AB

Printed in Great Britain

Dedications

For Tadhg and Alannah

Match day was here for the team in Littlesville.
Jake packed up his bag and ran to the hill,

Where the bus would be waiting for the team to hop on and begin their journey while they sang their team song.

'Hip hip hooray for the Littlesville Tigers! We're going to win this! We're the high flyers! We've done the practice, now it's our time. Let's show the world, just how we shine!'

Coach Robbie hopped on
and counted their heads
but soon stood still as he
looked on with dread.

'Nine players,' he cried.
'What will we do?'

'We can't play the
match when we
are missing two!'

'Who's missing?' Jake cried,
   as he looked round the bus.

'It's our star strikers Liam and Laura,
but let's not make a fuss!'

As Coach Robbie rang home to find out what was the story, Jake and his teammates started to feel poorly.

Coach Robbie came towards them and announced, 'It's the flu!' 'What will we do, guys, without our best two?

We have an hour until the match will begin. We can still figure out how we can win!'

The bus drove off and the team settled down;
not sure what to do, not making a sound.
When all of a sudden, Jake saw out the window,
a little boy his age kicking a ball – their hero!

'Stop the bus,' Jake called out. 'That boy over there!'
'Let's see if he'll join us. Let's hope that he'll care!'

Five minutes later, after a chat
between Coach and the boy's dad,
the boy hopped on the bus and
became the team's favourite lad!

'Now we have ten!' the team all cheered.
'We need one more,' Coach still feared.

As the bus sped on to get to the game,
the clock ticked on and the team began to tame.

What would they do? How would they win
the cup that they treasured? The chances were slim.

The bus slowed down to come to a stop;
outside the stadium, they heard a loud POP!
As the team looked around them, they noticed a girl first –
head down and teary – her football had burst.

Jake looked at Coach Robbie
and smiled as they realised
that their problem was no longer
– they needed to get organised.

Jake and the team ran to the changing room, while Coach Robbie went to sign up the newest member of their crew.

A fan of the Tigers – it was a perfect solution; she'd make a fantastic contribution!

The Tigers headed into the stadium for a pre-match walk around the pitch.

The players shook hands; and they took
their positions without a glitch.

Jake did his pre-match ritual: three hops and a jump;
his heart was beating fast with a thump thump thump.

'Hip hip hooray for the Littlesville Tigers!
We're going to win this! We're the high flyers!'

The fans' cheers shook the ground,
and the pre-match fireworks made a deafening sound.

The whistle was blown, and this was their time; some of the finest players of their generation ran up to the line.

The Tigers were on top, straight from the start;
it was clear that they were all playing their part.

Hernando was using all his dribbling skills as Coach Robbie reminded them of their training drills.

Murphy controlled the midfield, and the new players Alfie and Ariana formed a great defensive shield.

Up front, Savannah was a threat;
they were doing everything except putting the ball in the net.

Their shots hit the crossbar five times
– they tried their best,
and the Lakeside Leopards' goalkeeper
saved all the rest.

But the Tigers kept playing as a team;
with a smile on their faces,
they were still living their dream.

The referee blew the whistle for the end of the first half,
which came as a relief to the Lakeside coaching staff.

In the changing room, Coach Robbie gave a rousing speech, 'Boys and girls, this game is in our reach.'

The second half began;
the Tigers stuck to their plan.

But time slowly began running out,
while the fans from Littlesville began to doubt

– until the opposition gave a free kick away.

Could the Tigers make them pay?

It was Jake's turn to take the free kick; he went through the steps in his head really quick.

Three hops and a jump, and give the ball a mighty **whump**.

His heart beat fast with
a thump thump **thump**;

he stepped up, didn't flinch
and executed the free kick to an inch.

The Tigers had done it... Or so it seemed;
the ref wanted to check the TV screens.
They waited nervously until it was agreed,
they had scored deservedly.

One nil to Littlesville! What a goal, what a thrill.

Shortly after, the final whistle went;
the team and the fans were more than content.

'Hip hip hooray for
the Littlesville Tigers!
We've won our first game.
We're the high flyers!'

Milton Keynes UK
Ingram Content Group UK Ltd.
UKHW050012211123
432927UK00009B/184